Max and Emmy's Flower Power

I wish, I wish
With all my heart
To fly with dragons
In a land apart.

By Irene Trimble
Illustrated by The Thompson Brothers
Based on the characters by Ron Rodecker

A Random House PICTUREBACK® Shape Book
Random House 🏠 New York
Text and illustrations copyright © 2001 Sesame Workshop. Dragon Tales logo and characters ™ & © 2001
Sesame Workshop/Columbia TriStar Television Distribution. All rights reserved under International and
Pan-American Copyright Conventions. Published in the United States by Random House, Inc., New York,
and simultaneously in Canada by Random House of Canada Limited, Toronto, in conjunction with Sesame Workshop.
Sesame Workshop and its logos are trademarks and service marks of Sesame Workshop.
PICTUREBACK, RANDOM HOUSE, and the Random House colophon are registered trademarks of Random House, Inc.
Library of Congress Catalog Card Number: 00-103520 ISBN: 0-375-81156-7
www.randomhouse.com/kids/sesame
Visit Dragon Tales on the Web at www.dragontales.com
Printed in the United States of America January 2001 10 9 8 7 6 5 4 3 2

One day in the magical playroom, Emmy was busy
marking little potted plants with a crayon.

"There!" she told her little brother, Max. "Now we can
tell our plants apart."

"Oh, it'll be easy to tell which is mine," cried Max. "It'll
be the one growing up to the sky!"

"Only if you water it," Emmy reminded him.

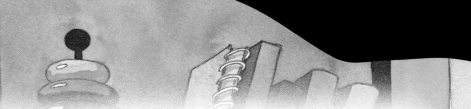

Suddenly, the magic dragon scale in the window seat began to shimmer and glow.

"The dragons are calling us!" cried Max. "Let's go!"

In a whirl of sparkles, Max and Emmy found themselves in a jungle of giant plants.

"Are we in Dragon Land?" asked Max.

"Of course!" answered Ord. Their big dragon friend popped out from behind a huge sack of magic plant food. "These are my sunflowers for the Flower Festival plant contest!"

"Ord, are your flowers supposed to be *this* big?" asked Emmy as the thick stems grew taller and taller.

"Maybe I'm feeding them a little too much," said Ord. "I'll worry about that later. Right now I'm busy building a trophy case for when I win first prize!"

Max peered around a tall sunflower for a look at
the case—and accidentally bumped into the towering flower!
"Watch it, buddy!" the sunflower yelled as it fell over with a
loud CRASH!
"Hey!" someone cried. "That almost squashed my two-lips!"
Max, Emmy, and Ord followed the voice until they came upon
their friends Zak and Wheezie.

"Did you say tulips, Zak?" asked Max. "All I see are weeds!"
"Oh, I'll pull out those pesky bugleweeds later," Zak
answered, fussing with some papers. "Right now I have to
practice my speech for when I win first prize in the contest."

"Save your dragon breath, Zaky! First prize belongs to me!" said Wheezie. "My champion daffy-dils tell silly jokes when they're happy."

"They don't *look* very happy now," said Emmy. "Do they need more sunlight?"

"Oh, I don't know," Wheezie replied. "I've been too busy looking for the perfect hat to wear to the contest!"

"Hi, everyone!" cried Cassie as she swooped in for a landing. "I just got all these neat gardening books from the library! There's one about a Great Gardener Dragon. He lives in the sky and knows everything about growing flowers. I'm going to keep reading so I can win the contest."

CLARA
FILL

FLOWER

"Um, Cassie, what kind of flowers did you plant?" asked Max.

"Dancing daisies," answered Cassie.

"You mean like those daisies that are waltzing away?" asked Emmy.

"My daisies! Why are they leaving?" cried Cassie.

"Did you water them today?" Max asked Cassie.

"Oh, no!" exclaimed Cassie. "I was so busy reading I forgot!"

"Look!" said Max, pointing up to the sky. All of Cassie's dancing daisies, Zak's two-lips, and Wheezie's daffy-dils were climbing one of Ord's giant sunflowers. They soon disappeared into the clouds.

"Holy honeysuckle!" cried Wheezie. "Now *all* of our plants are running away!"

"Maybe if we hurry, we can catch up to them!" said Max as he jumped onto one of the gigantic sunflower stems and began to climb.

"You lead the way, Max!" said Emmy, scampering up, too. The children and the dragons quickly followed the flowers into the sky.

Max and Emmy climbed higher and higher. Finally, their heads popped up through a puffy cloud.

"Wow! That must be the Great Gardener Dragon," whispered Emmy.

"Look!" cried Ord. "My sunflowers are here—and they're shining!"

"My two-lips are here, too," said Zak, "and they're singing!"

"My little daffy-dils are laughing!" squealed Wheezie.

"And my dancing daisies are doing a jig!" cried Cassie.

"Your garden is great!" Max told the Great Gardener Dragon. "I'll bet it's because you use magic!"

"Or is it your green thumbs?" Emmy giggled.

"You don't need magic or a green thumb to grow things!" laughed the dragon. "Flowers come here because they need someone to take care of them."

"I should've weeded my garden," said Zak, "instead of worrying about giving a speech at the contest."

"And *I* should have spent more time watering my flowers," added Cassie sadly.

"If we promise to take super-good care of them," Wheezie asked, "do you think our flowers will come home with us?"

"Let's ask them," said the Great Gardener Dragon.

"Knock, knock," a daffy-dil said.

"Who's there?" answered Emmy.

"Orange," said the little flower.

"Orange who?" asked Max.

"Orange you glad we said yes?"

"Looove it!" cried Wheezie.

"Don't forget," called out the Great Gardener Dragon. "You must take care of living things that need you—then *everyone* will be a winner!"

"Yippee!" yelled Ord. "Let's go home and get ready for the contest!"

"I think it's time for us to go home, too," Emmy said as she and Max waved good-bye.

When the children returned to their playroom, Max hurried over to his thirsty little plant and gave it a big drink of water.

"Look, Emmy! I'm taking care of my plant!" Max cried.

Emmy smiled. "Now, that gets a big green thumbs-up!"